To Mahmoud
who told me this story

The publishers acknowledge generous assistance from
the Ontario Arts Council and the Canada Council.

© 1995 Text Shenaaz Nanji

© 1995 Illustrations Shahd Shaker

CANADIAN CATALOGUING IN PUBLICATION DATA

Nanji, Shenaaz
    The old fisherman of Lamu

ISBN 0-920661-53-X

I. Shaker, Shahd.   II. Title.

PS8577.A57305 1995   j398.2'09676   C95-932510-7
PZ8.1.N3501 1995

TSAR Publications
P.O. Box 6996, Station A, Toronto, Ontario, Canada   M5W 1X7

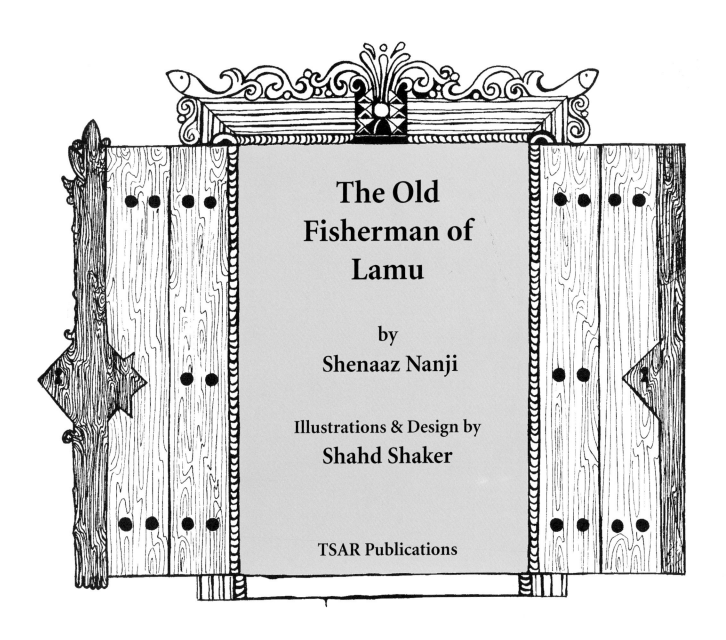

The Old Fisherman of Lamu

by

Shenaaz Nanji

Illustrations & Design by

Shahd Shaker

TSAR Publications

Lamu island lay tucked like a pearl in an oyster, way behind earth's back. Here lived the old fisherman Mzee, with his ancient mtepe-dhow (a boat he used for fishing), and his young friend Toto. Everyday at noon, when the sun broke out fiercely in the sky, Mzee stopped fishing and lay under the mango tree dreaming dreams.

Many people thought Mzee was strange and lazy.

"The sun has gotten into his head and turned him crazy," muttered the women draped in black veils who sold fish and vegetables at the market.

"He has the bones and blood of a donkey," snubbed the coffee-seller pouring steaming black coffee to the women.

Toto and Mzee would play bao together. Counting and shifting the stones on the board, Mzee read the blue seas. He spoke the rise and fall of tides, the coming of storms and monsoons.

As darkness fell, he read the black skies. Gazing at the twinkling stars, he spoke of the drought and the coming of Mzungu the strange man from across the sea.

One day before sunset Mzee took Toto in his boat, the mtepe-dhow. The stormy sea was roaring rough. The farther they went the rougher it became. The waves leaped and fell, the little boat was tossed up and down on the sea.

Suddenly Mzee whistled a strange tune. Immediately the sea lost its fury and became calm and clear like a sheet of blue glass.

Under the sea Toto saw the other world. Coral, shells and schools of fish dressed in the colours of a rainbow; flowers glittering and glowing like stars in heaven.

Plop! Splash! Plop! A school of fish, the chungu, nguru, kile-kole, and danfu flew in and out of the water, flapping their fins like dancers. The sea changed into creamy foam and froth. The fish were all under Mzee's spell, they awaited his command. Toto was lost in wonder.

A few days later Mzungu, the strange man from across the ocean, arrived. Throngs of people flocked to hear Mzungu. Toto's heart raced as he too pushed his way to see the man.

Standing high on a wooden crate, Mzungu thundered:
"I will make your dreams come true!"
"Mzungu! Mzungu!" sang the crowd in unison.

Eyeing old Mzee napping under the Mango tree, Mzungu cried out:
"Wake up, old man, there's treasure in the sea!"
     All faces turned towards Mzee.
     But Mzee did not twitch a muscle.

But to everyone's surprise, Toto's voice rang out:

"Mzee reads the skies. He reads the seas.
Mzee is magic. He talks to the fishes."

The people shook their heads in disbelief, whispering
"That Mzee has bewitched poor little Toto."

Toto went on:

"*Mzee catches ten fishes. He keeps five, sells five.*
  Five is what he needs,
    But he can catch as many as he wishes..."

"Mzee should throw his old palm-rib fishing rod!" roared Mzungu. Mzee's old palm-rib fishing rod had seen strong winds and high waves, it had helped Mzee to feed his wife and four daughters.

"How will Mzee feed his wife and four daughters?" Toto asked.

"Use a spiffy new fishing net!" Mzungu said.

"With a fishing rod catch one fish at a time,
    With a fishing net catch hundreds at a time!"

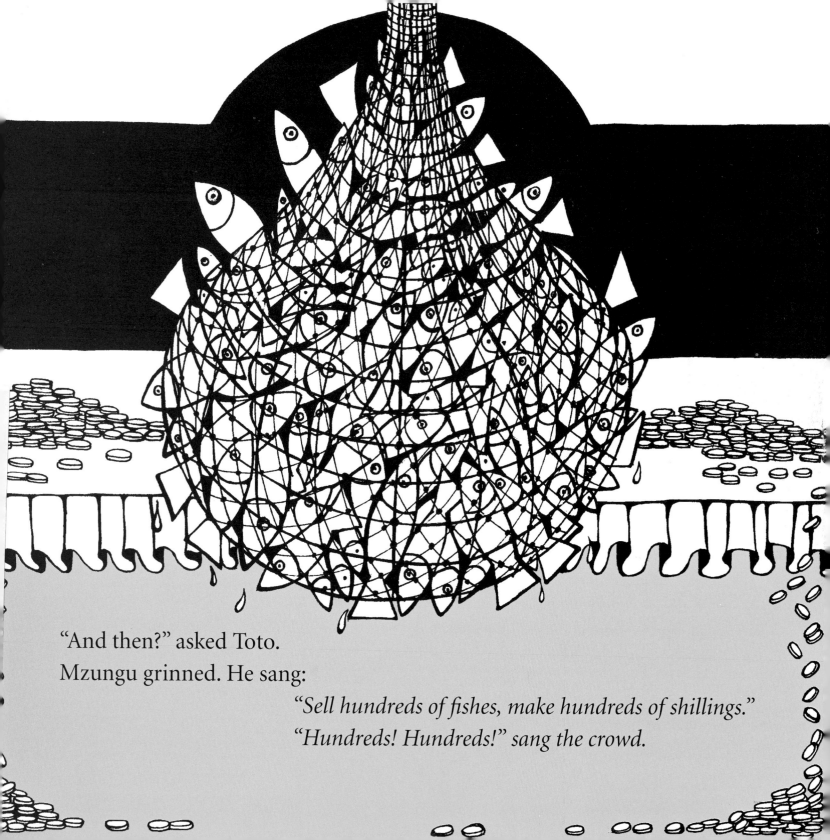

"And then?" asked Toto.
Mzungu grinned. He sang:

      "*Sell hundreds of fishes, make hundreds of shillings.*"
      "*Hundreds! Hundreds!*" sang the crowd.

"And then?" asked Toto.
"Throw away and sink Mzee's old weary mtepe-dhow," said Mzungu.

Toto thought of the boat that took him and Mzee to the other world. It was made from coconut fibre and wood. It had taken Mzee many days and many nights to make it. Mzee loved it.

"Buy a motor boat," said Mzungu. He sang,
"*The motor boat with its engine is bigger and better!*
Bigger and better, goes farther and faster!
Farther and faster, catch thousands of fishes,
sell thousands of fishes, make thousands of shillings!"

"Thousands! Thousands!" roared the crowd.

"What will Mzee do with all
the money?" Toto asked.
"Buy a fleet of motor boats,"
sang Mzungu.

"Cover even more seas,
catch millions of fishes,
sell millions of fishes,
make millions of shillings!"

"Millions! Millions!"
thundered
the crowd.

"And then?" asked Toto.

"Then Mzee will have a fish factory. He'll hire workers. He'll be the boss." Mzungu grinned.

"Mzungu! Mzungu!" sang the crowd.

"What will Mzee do then?" Toto asked.

"Ho ho ho!" Mzungu laughed. "Then Mzee stops fishing. He sits. He rests. He sleeps."

"But what is Mzee doing now?" Toto asked.

All the faces turned towards Mzee.

The old man was lying under the mango tree sleeping, his kofia-hat on his face hiding his toothless smile.

And if in your travels you come across the harbour of Lamu some day, you may see old Mzee dreaming dreams under the mango tree taking shade from the fierce afternoon sun.

Know then that he has all he wishes.

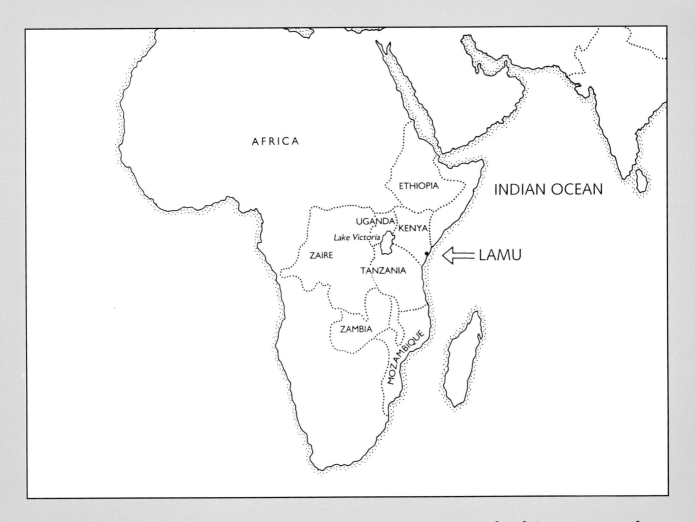

Lamu is an ancient island town on the east coast of Africa, somewhat north of Mombasa in Kenya. It has a long and colourful history of more than a thousand years, and is renowned for its beautiful carved doors, its wonderful poetry and its dhows. The mtepe-dhow was made of planks held together with ropes and had no nails. In olden times Lamu was an important town, where dhow-making was a way of life. Nowadays Lamu is simply a small beautiful town of narrow streets and old houses, and it has no cars!